THIS AWESOME BOOK
BELONGS TO:

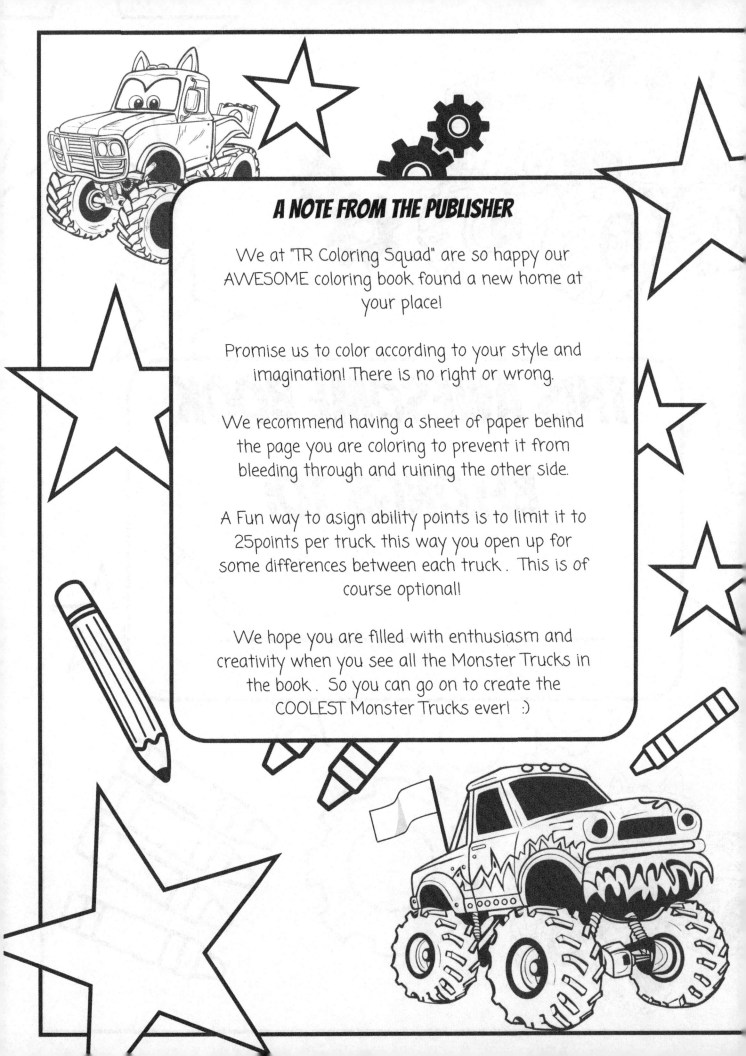

A NOTE FROM THE PUBLISHER

We at "TR Coloring Squad" are so happy our AWESOME coloring book found a new home at your place!

Promise us to color according to your style and imagination! There is no right or wrong.

We recommend having a sheet of paper behind the page you are coloring to prevent it from bleeding through and ruining the other side.

A Fun way to asign ability points is to limit it to 25points per truck this way you open up for some differences between each truck. This is of course optional!

We hope you are filled with enthusiasm and creativity when you see all the Monster Trucks in the book. So you can go on to create the COOLEST Monster Trucks ever! :)

TRUCK NAME : _____

STATS

POWER   AIR   SPEED   STUNTS   STAMINA

TRUCK NAME : _____

STATS

POWER   **AIR**   **SPEED**   **STUNTS**   **STAMINA**

STATS

POWER   AIR   SPEED   STUNTS   STAMINA

TRUCK NAME : _____

STATS

POWER   **AIR**   **SPEED**   **STUNTS**   **STAMINA**

TRUCK NAME : _____

STATS

| POWER | AIR | SPEED | STUNTS | STAMINA |

STATS

POWER   AIR   SPEED   STUNTS   STAMINA

STATS

POWER	AIR	SPEED	STUNTS	STAMINA

TRUCK NAME : _____

TRUCK NAME : _____

STATS

POWER   AIR   SPEED   STUNTS   STAMINA

TRUCK NAME:

STATS

POWER AIR SPEED STUNTS STAMINA

TRUCK NAME : _____

STATS

POWER   **AIR**   **SPEED**   **STUNTS**   **STAMINA**

TRUCK NAME:

STATS

POWER	AIR	SPEED	STUNTS	STAMINA

TRUCK NAME : _____

STATS

POWER

AIR

SPEED

STUNTS

STAMINA

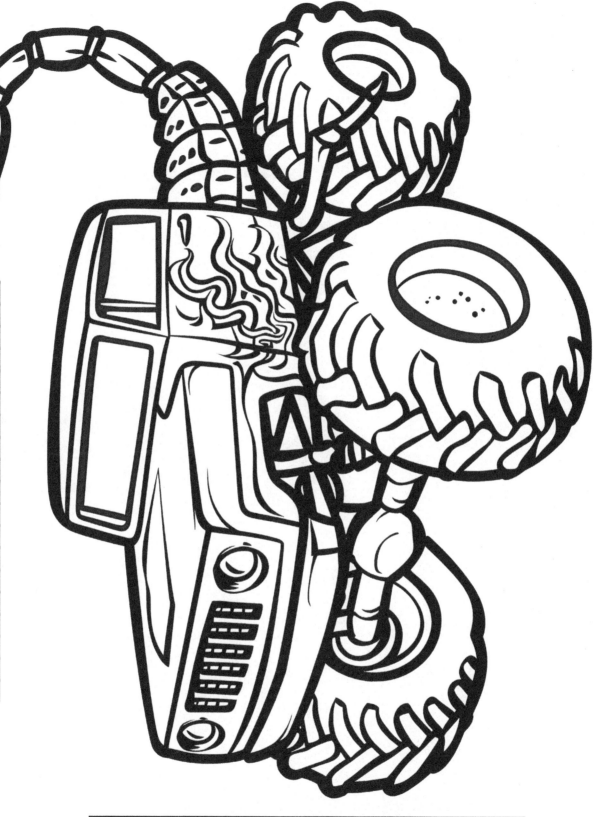

TRUCK NAME :

STATS

POWER

AIR

SPEED

STUNTS

STAMINA

TRUCK NAME : _____

STATS

| POWER | AIR | SPEED | STUNTS | STAMINA |

TRUCK NAME:

STATS

POWER   AIR   SPEED   STUNTS   STAMINA

TRUCK NAME : _____

STATS

POWER   AIR   SPEED   STUNTS   STAMINA

TRUCK NAME : _____

STATS

POWER   **AIR**   **SPEED**   **STUNTS**   **STAMINA**

STATS

POWER   **AIR**   **SPEED**   **STUNTS**   **STAMINA**

TRUCK NAME : _____

STATS

POWER

AIR

SPEED

STUNTS

STAMINA

TRUCK NAME : _____

STATS

POWER

AIR

SPEED

STUNTS

STAMINA

TRUCK NAME :

STATS

| POWER | AIR | SPEED | STUNTS | STAMINA |

TRUCK NAME : _____

TRUCK NAME : _____

STATS

POWER   **AIR**   **SPEED**   **STUNTS**   **STAMINA**

TRUCK NAME :

STATS

POWER AIR STUNTS SPEED STAMINA

TRUCK NAME : _____

STATS

POWER   AIR   SPEED   STUNTS   STAMINA

POWER   AIR   SPEED   STUNTS   STAMINA

TRUCK NAME : _____

STATS

POWER   AIR   SPEED   STUNTS   STAMINA

STATS

POWER ▱▱▱▱▱▱▱

AIR ▱▱▱▱▱▱▱

SPEED ▱▱▱▱▱▱▱

STUNTS ▱▱▱▱▱▱▱

STAMINA ▱▱▱▱▱▱▱

TRUCK NAME :

TRUCK NAME : _____

STATS

| POWER | AIR | SPEED | STUNTS | STAMINA |

TRUCK NAME:

STATS
POWER   AIR   SPEED   STUNTS   STAMINA

TRUCK NAME : _____

STATS

| POWER | AIR | SPEED | STUNTS | STAMINA |

| POWER | AIR | SPEED | STUNTS | STAMINA |

TRUCK NAME : _____

TRUCK NAME : _____

STATS

| POWER | AIR | SPEED | STUNTS | STAMINA |

TRUCK NAME : _____

STATS

POWER   AIR   SPEED   STUNTS   STAMINA

TRUCK NAME : _____

STATS

| POWER | AIR | SPEED | STUNTS | STAMINA |

TRUCK NAME : _____

STATS

| POWER | AIR | SPEED | STUNTS | STAMINA |

STATS

POWER   AIR   SPEED   STUNTS   STAMINA

TRUCK NAME : _____

TRUCK NAME :

STATS

POWER
▯▯▯▯▯▯▯▯

AIR
▯▯▯▯▯▯▯▯

SPEED
▯▯▯▯▯▯▯▯

STUNTS
▯▯▯▯▯▯▯▯

STAMINA
▯▯▯▯▯▯▯▯

STATS

POWER	AIR	SPEED	STUNTS	STAMINA

TRUCK NAME : _____

STATS

POWER	AIR	SPEED	STUNTS	STAMINA

TRUCK NAME :

TRUCK NAME : _____

STATS

POWER □-□□□□□□□□

AIR □-□□□□□□□□

SPEED □-□□□□□□□□

STUNTS □-□□□□□□□□

STAMINA □-□□□□□□□□

POWER **AIR** **SPEED** **STUNTS** **STAMINA**

TRUCK NAME : _____

STATS

POWER ▱▱▱▱▱▱▱▱▱▱
AIR ▱▱▱▱▱▱▱▱▱▱
SPEED ▱▱▱▱▱▱▱▱▱▱
STUNTS ▱▱▱▱▱▱▱▱▱▱
STAMINA ▱▱▱▱▱▱▱▱▱▱

TRUCK NAME :

TRUCK NAME : _____

STATS

POWER **AIR** **SPEED** **STUNTS** **STAMINA**

TRUCK NAME:

STATS

POWER AIR SPEED STUNTS STAMINA

TRUCK NAME : _____

STATS

POWER	AIR	SPEED	STUNTS	STAMINA

STATS

POWER   AIR   SPEED   STUNTS   STAMINA

TRUCK NAME : _____

STATS

POWER	AIR	SPEED	LIGHTS	STAMINA

TRUCK NAME:

TRUCK NAME : _____

STATS

POWER   AIR   SPEED   STUNTS   STAMINA

TRUCK NAME :

STATS

POWER ⬜⬜⬜⬜⬜⬜⬜

AIR ⬜⬜⬜⬜⬜⬜⬜

SPEED ⬜⬜⬜⬜⬜⬜⬜

STUNTS ⬜⬜⬜⬜⬜⬜⬜

STAMINA ⬜⬜⬜⬜⬜⬜⬜

STATS

POWER   AIR   SPEED   STUNTS   STAMINA

TRUCK NAME : _____

TRUCK NAME :

STATS

POWER

AIR

SPEED

STUNTS

STAMINA

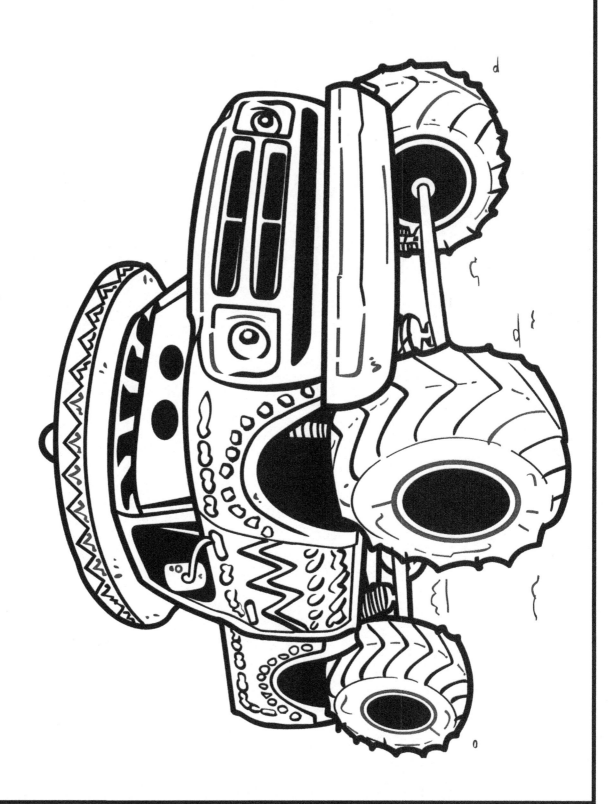

TRUCK NAME : _____

STATS

POWER   AIR   SPEED   STUNTS   STAMINA

TRUCK NAME : _____

STATS

POWER

AIR

SPEED

STUNTS

STAMINA

TRUCK NAME:

STATS

POWER AIR SPEED STUNTS STAMINA

TRUCK NAME : _____

STATS

POWER   AIR   SPEED   STUNTS   STAMINA

STATS

POWER | AIR | SPEED | STUNTS | STEERING

TRUCK NAME : _____

STATS

POWER   AIR   SPEED   STUNTS   STAMINA

STATS

POWER   AIR   SPEED   STUNTS   STAMINA

TRUCK NAME : _____

TRUCK NAME : _____

STATS

POWER

AIR

SPEED

STUNTS

STAMINA

STATS

POWER AIR SPEED STUNTS STAMINA

TRUCK NAME : _____

STATS

POWER   AIR   SPEED   STUNTS   STAMINA

TRUCK NAME : _____

STATS

POWER   AIR   SPEED   STUNTS   STAMINA

TRUCK NAME : _____

TRUCK NAME :

STATS

POWER

AIR

SPEED

STUNTS

STAMINA

STATS

POWER ▫▫▫▫▫▫▫▫▯▯▯

AIR ▫▫▫▫▫▫▫▫▯▯▯

SPEED ▫▫▫▫▫▫▫▫▯▯▯

STUNTS ▫▫▫▫▫▫▫▫▯▯▯

STAMINA ▫▫▫▫▫▫▫▫▯▯▯

TRUCK NAME : _____

STATS

POWER

AIR

SPEED

STUNTS

STAMINA

TRUCK NAME!

TRUCK NAME :

STATS

POWER

AIR

SPEED

STUNTS

STAMINA

POWER   AIR   SPEED   STUNTS   STAMINA

TRUCK NAME : _____

Made in the USA
Coppell, TX
23 November 2024

40862532R00063